Children of the White Rider

Written By
Sean Hunt

The continuing adventures of The White Rider

This book is a work of fiction.
Original characters and their names are fictitious.
Any resemblance to actual persons, living or dead,
is coincidental. Some events and locations are inspired
by actual historical happenings, but all are presented in
an alternate history, fictitious format.

Printed in the United States of America

Published by Hunt House Books & Media
Written by Sean Hunt
Formatted and Edited by Kylie Hunt
Edited by Michaela Bush
Additional Edits by Bethany M. Griggs
Cover Design by Hunt Production Studios
Author Photo by The Film Director's Wife
Children of the White Rider book cover art by Dennis Bergen

ISBN: 979-8-234-04764-9

Children of the White Rider

The above artwork is illustrated by Dennis Bergen.

Setting: United States Territory

Date: 1890 Alternate American History

Ten years after the events of the first White Rider Novella

Relive the story and adventure of The White Rider Book Series

Children of the White Rider

Table of Contents

Children of the White Rider

Table of Contents

PROLOGUE Alternate Version of History

The White Rider, the first one to carry the mantle, was General William Maxwell. He was the central hero of the American Civil War on the Northern Union side. Winning the Civil War earlier than in recorded history —the war started in 1861 and concluded in 1864, instead of 1865, at the Battle of Gettysburg—a battle now lasting ten days and concluding the conflict one year earlier than in regular recorded American history.

The White Rider and President Abraham Lincoln spent the next year forcing the remnant of Southern Confederacy Resistance into submission and to accept their defeat. The White Rider, General William Maxwell, helped save President Abraham Lincoln from assassination at the Ford Theater in 1865.

It was revealed that John Wilkes Booth had been paid by the sinister, two-faced Grisham family to assassinate President Lincoln.

In retaliation for saving Lincoln's life, the villain Malcolm Grisham, in an attempt to humiliate his rival, arranged for the demotion of General Maxwell to Colonel and successfully executed Maxwell's demise, which shook the United States.

The White Rider's son, Chapman, was framed for the murder of his father, imprisoned, and sold into slavery as property of Bounty Hunter Dugg Roanan. Eventually, Chapman was set free, but that's another story.

Before imprisonment, Chapman had wedded Mary in 1862 in the midst of the Civil War, and bore Gracie Gail, who was secretly raised by the Reverend Henry Gail of the town of Conlin.

Chapman and Mary had two more children later on, and they were raised secretly by Mary far from the knowledge of anyone in a cabin in secluded American territory. To keep them safe, no one, not even the Grisham family knew that the two children existed and were alive for a decade.

The children grew for ten years and then were discovered as the Children of the White Rider, when our story takes place at the hidden cabin in 1890.

This is the story of Chapman's two young children who become hunted by the descendants of the sinister and devious Grisham family.

Set in alternate history 1890, what follows is a daring and exciting adventure that the whole family will enjoy reading. Find out what happens in this wagon-wheel, edge of your seat, old-fashioned escapade tale in the White Rider Series. Enjoy reading the new adventure, Children of The White Rider.

A DARK CONVERSATION AT REK INC.

"We cannot let the children of the White Rider get away, much less live."

"Why, boss?"

"Because, dummy, they're like weeds, you let one alone and then you'll have them all over the place. If they live, they spread seeds of hope to the poor and needy. We could probably handle one at a time, but we cannot allow the hope of the White Rider to survive. That hope will ignite, and that's not what we want because it will spread. Do you understand, my boy?"

"Yeah, boss. How many men do we send after them?"

"Send them all."

"Yes, boss."

WHAT'S THIS NEW ADVENTURE ABOUT?

Morgan and Katherine find out what they're made of and their heritage in adventure and faith as the children of the White Rider.

Roanan helps guide them and tries to keep them out of mischief and trouble.

Children of the Grisham family are hot on their tail. The Grishams are determined to stop the children of the White Rider before they can become who they are meant to be.

"We cannot wait for tomorrow to come. We have to do something now." Morgan was determined.

ABOUT THE CHILDREN OF THE WHITE RIDER

Morgan and his sister were always getting into trouble. Morgan refused to work as a team.

His sister and Roanan were always telling him he needed to be willing to accept help.

Morgan was far too headstrong and stubborn to allow anyone to help him.

This led to time and time again of misadventures and trouble, where the call of their father's legacy led Morgan and Katherine into an epic journey and adventure of a lifetime.

The adventures of TWR continue with Children of the White Rider.

THE GRISHAM CHILDREN

The Grisham family marriages were usually arranged and filled with lies and empty promises by the mother-in-laws spinning and building lives of emptiness to their dark heart's desires. Schemes. Plans within plans. Their weddings were like witch coven meetings.

Dark spells cast to solidify and hold a new dark age for each of the children, who paid for their false illusion of lies. Making dirty and devious back room deals.

Six children meant six dark deals when the wedding bells rang.

GRISHAM'S FAMILY FEAST

After their corrupt family attended church services on Sunday mornings, the Grishams would meet at one of their family houses, where they would forget to thank the Lord and ask Him to bless a bountiful feast that was mostly stolen, bribed, and obtained illegally.

One of the Grisham children that had a mostly good heart realized his family ate like sinister pigs. It destroyed his appetite and disgusted him enough to grab a bare minimum and finish his meal outside.

"I don't want to be a pig," said the boy.

"Pigging out is what we do," replied the Grishams.

They stole from several families who rented cabins from their family.

They would break in and take their food.

“You cannot do this, this is our food! If you take this, we will starve!” the families cried.

“No rent, no food. Not our problem,” was the Grishams’ cold reply.

A GLIMPSE OF WHAT IS TO COME

“That’s just a senile old man,” yelled Morgan.

“What does senile mean?” asked Katherine.

“It means he’s crazy!” shouted Morgan.

“Wait, what’s he doing?” asked Katherine.

“That crazy old man is…” began Morgan, but before he could explain any further, old man Roanan pulled open his weapon carrying case full of parts and pieces of a silver and wooden rifle.

“That crazy old man is about to save our lives,” concluded a confident Morgan concerning the situation.

“What?!” asked Katherine.

They both watched as the old man Roanan quickly and expertly assembled his silver rifle and eliminated one bad guy after another. About fifteen altogether.

“See, told ya,” said a happy-with-himself Morgan.

The men who were shot were all alive, just lying on the ground, groaning and moaning.

“The White Rider don’t believe in killing,” said Katherine.

“I didn’t,” Roanan said.

“What did he say?” asked Morgan.

“He ain’t killing,” said Katherine.

“From dust you came and to dust you shall return, so long, Grishams!” Katherine proudly stated.

OLD MAN ROANAN IS ON THE CASE

Old man Dugg Roanan had a lot more white hairs than he'd had just ten years prior when he was riding by the side of the second White Rider, Chapman, in 1880. They had fought many foes, won many battles, gone on many adventures, and none of them had really scared him, except for almost drowning several times. He'd finally learned how to swim.

He had visited the local town to restock on supplies, especially ammunition for his white and silver rifle that had an amazing silver scope on it. He had gone to the telegram office to send word to his wife that he was headed home soon after the supply run, but he was not able to finish sending his telegram when an urgent message came in for him, seemingly out of the blue.

"Are you old man Dugg Roanan?" asked the elder telegram operator.

“None other,” said Dugg Roanan.

“Well, you have a message,” said the telegram operator.

Dugg Roanan was excited. “Let’s hear it!”

“It’s from a Gracie Gail Emerson. Do you know her?” asked the telegram operator.

Of course Roanan knew her; she was the eldest daughter of his best friend, Chapman, the White Rider.

Roanan took the paper message and read it to himself. “Children of Chapman in trouble. No one to protect them. They are headed to see me. Help them make it.” Roanan paused. He knew a great adventure was about to begin and that if he was not careful, all of the fresh milk that he had just purchased was going to spoil.

PREFACE

The mother of the two children had disappeared a week earlier.

She had said it had been on urgent business. She also said that if people they did not know arrived at the cabin looking for them, they needed to leave immediately and head to their elder sister Gracie Gail's house, which was very far away from them.

Go to their older sister's home for safety, is what Morgan could remember. They needed to take enough food and supplies to last for at least a three-week journey.

The children were not for sure where Gracie Gail Emerson was at, but they knew there were good odds that she was living in Conlin, where their mother, Mary, had mentioned that she was a school teacher.

IT BEGINS

Morgan and Katherine stood outside of their house as a dark, tall figure approached.

He was on a black horse, and the tall, dark figure got off the black horse. He slowly made his way over to the house to Morgan and Katherine.

Morgan stood next to Katherine. They both looked at each other, as if they weren't sure what to make out of the figure of the dark man, but they both had a sense that he was not there for their well-being.

"I knew your mother. I knew your father. I'm an old friend of your family," said the tall, dark figure.

Somehow, he seemed insincere and untruthful, Morgan thought.

Katherine thought the same thing. Mother told her and Morgan to be careful of strangers. Especially ones who were strange, like the tall, dark figure. They could smell him several yards away, so they already knew that he had poor hygiene. This was not a good start to the tall, dark figure who had been sent by the Grisham family. It was not a good start for him, at all.

"I just want to talk to you for a little bit, for a few moments," the tall mysterious man said. Morgan and Katherine were unconvinced.
"I was friends, I was friends with the White Rider, your father," he continued.

Morgan now knew for sure that he was not telling the truth. The tall, dark man with the dark horse figured by now that the two were not buying what he was selling.

So he moved to plan B. Not the smartest, but he still moved to it. He drew his pistols, two of them, and took aim at both Morgan and Katherine.

The two children, who had already sensed that this might go the way that it was unfolding, dove behind two wine barrels by the house.

The tall, dark man began to move. He cursed. “I missed. They won’t be too happy about this. They said quick and easy.” He knew now that it was going to be the complete opposite, but he had been sent there on a mission to kidnap the children of the White Rider. He was going to leave with his prize, one way or another.

“What do you think he wants?” yelled Katherine to Morgan.

Morgan was already inside grabbing and loading his gun, a rifle that he had been gifted on a birthday earlier.

He said very quickly, “I don’t think we need to stick around to find out. They’re not here for our good. Mother warned us one day they might come for us. It’s time to get going.”

Katherine was not going to follow those directions. She wasn’t being agreeable today.

“I will not leave. This is our home; we have to stay and fight for it. We have to stay! It’s what Mother would have wanted,” she said.

Morgan turned back, very sternly faced Katherine, and grabbed her by the arm.

“Mother is not here right now, Katherine. We have to go, and go now. He’s just the first. My gut tells me he’s the first of many. We have to save ourselves—we have to go and hide,” he said.

“Hide! That’s the opposite of what the White Rider would do. Mother told us…” Katherine began.

Morgan cut her off. “Like I said, Mother’s not here right now, and the White Rider, we can’t do anything in his name or continue his legacy if we’re both six feet under in the ground, can we?” he asked.

Katherine shook her head with tears coming to her eyes and down her cheeks.

“No,” Katherine said. “I suppose not.”

“Then, it’s time to go.” said Morgan, who was already five steps ahead of the bad guy and everyone else. He’d always had that gut drive, that gut feeling, and now it was coming into fruition. He was putting it into action, for he knew he had to do something.

He had to take care of Katherine and the situation, even if he was just ten years old. The children of the White Rider would survive that day.

“Hurry, quick, hurry! Let’s go, let’s go!” Morgan shouted at Katherine.

Katherine was still dragging her feet. Katherine ran to get her mother's frying pan and pack it with her getaway bag. Katherine frantically looked for her doll next.

"Why are you bringing a doll and Mother's frying pan?" asked a stumped Morgan.

"For war," Katherine said, referencing the pan and—for love—referencing her doll.

"I thought you were going to say for food," said Morgan.

Katherine was too busy to respond. She finally found the doll, and was now leaving the cabin rather quickly after Morgan continued to push and push, but Katherine kept dropping her things, including the doll.

“What’s going on? What is happening? Can someone tell me? What is happening? What are we going to do? Where are we going to go?” yelled Katherine as Morgan had their packed bags and they were running through the back woods.

Now, the man in black with the black horse had no idea that Morgan and Katherine were that far ahead of him. He was still searching the cabin, their house that they had just deserted.

Morgan was making his way with Katherine as fast and as far as possible to the back river. He and Katherine were going to get in a boat that they’d used for fishing earlier on. Morgan had somehow already been planning an escape. It was something that his mother had told him that he might need to be aware of and ready to do one day.

As much as his rebellious self wanted to ignore his mother's advice, he knew that she was right. Who was he to question the mother of the children of the White Rider or the wife of the White Rider? They felt the White Rider's presence here and there in their family over the years, though only pictures of him survived. Supposedly, the White Rider, their father, had given his life to protect a small group of settlers, who were at the hands of the sinister Apache. Chapman had tried to prevent another war, as this was only twenty years after the Civil War.

Chapman and Roanan had been successful, however, Chapman had given his life to save the settlers, Roanan, and everyone there.

THE BOAT

Morgan and Katherine made it to the boat successfully. The boat, carrying the two children, was off and in the water, headed far from where they had lived for most of their lives.

The tall black figure made his way to the pier and aimed his large, black pistol at the children. He cocked the firearm and prepared to fire. When he pulled the trigger, he suddenly collapsed and fell into the stream.

When the body submerged, the children looked back to see the tall black man gone, and in his place, several hundred yards behind him, was another figure, a much, much older, shorter man with a beard as white as snow. This man was dressed in a long white and brown trench coat.

He stood firm like a bear on the hillside with a long white and silver rifle. Now that the children were safe, the white and brown bear disappeared, at least at this time.

The children didn't know it, but they had a guardian angel, a protector on their side.

Perhaps more than one, even, thought Morgan to himself.

For now, as the boat picked up speed and made its way down the stream, the two children could take a moment to rest.

What new dangers awaited them? Only God knew, and they were going to have to trust God to help them make it through this turbulent and dangerous situation.

"Mom said to go to the mountain, remember. That's what she said, Morgan. Go to the mountain if we ever had to leave the cabin," Katherine said.

"I know what she said, Katherine. But Mom's not here, and we're not going to the mountain. At least...not right now. Not till later, after I can figure out what is going," replied Morgan.

A gunshot was heard!

"Mother would say, 'working for or with the Grisham family is a nightmare that never ends and never gets better.' She also said to only trust a Grisham as far as you can throw them," was Katherine's reply. "We can't throw them at all; we're small children, Morgan."

"Exactly," said Morgan with a smile.

"What do they want from us, brother?" Katherine asked Morgan.

"If I had to guess, they're planning something. Something big, and they need anyone who could be a problem for them out of the way," was his reply.

"Who and what?" asked Katherine.

"The Grishams, Katherine. They've always had it out for the family of the White Rider," he told her.

"What do they want to do?" she asked.

"Something they ain't supposed to do. Could be anything, but it most likely has to do with power and money. They love that sort of thing," Morgan said.

Morgan looked down at a piece of paper he had torn away from the tall, dark man, who had come to their home and chased them earlier. The tall, dark man had grabbed ahold of Morgan's arm, and in an attempt to break free, Morgan had kicked and grabbed something in the sinister man's belt: a piece of paper.

The piece of paper said Rek Inc. on it. It was a pay stub. The tall, dark man, with insidious intentions for the children, had worked for Rek Inc., the construction company building rock barriers in the area for a decade.

"Rek Incorporated has been working on constructing a dam barrier for a decade now," Morgan said.

"Woe to you, Morgan. Watch your language," said a stern Katherine. She would say she was concerned, but her brother thought that most things she did that bothered him could be classified as stern.

"I wasn't using it in a curse-like manner," he said.

"Yes, but you still should be careful," was her reply. "How do you know all this about the Grishams?" she asked Morgan.

"Mom," Morgan was quick to answer.

“What did she tell you?” asked a confused Katherine.

“Everything,” said a confident Morgan.

“Everything?” said Katherine, even more confused now.

“Everything I need to know,” he confirmed.

“For what?” she asked.

“To survive,” he replied.

Where do we survive and go now? Morgan had already been pondering this. He’d figured their only hope at the moment was to go to their elder sister Gracie’s place.

“Why her?” asked Katherine.

“If the Grishams are hunting us, and it sure looks that way, elder sister Gracie is one of the only safe places we can go at this time,” he told her.

“All right, sounds like a plan. Let’s go,” said Katherine.

"That was easy. Usually, it takes a ton more convincing to get you to do anything," said a relieved Morgan.

"I know, but at this time..." Katherine started.

"Yes..." Morgan quickly said.

"I'm trying to be better," stated an exhausted Katherine.

"That's...that's good," said a confused Morgan. Morgan laughed.

"I am glad my self-improvement amuses you," said an upset Katherine.

"Yeah." Morgan laughed once again. "It does." Morgan laughed many more times.

They continued on until the children made it to the train station.

"Two tickets for Conlin, please," Morgan said as he paid for their train tickets.

"Mother said never to go back to Conlin," said a determined Katherine.

"Yes, but she told us to get to our older sister Gracie if we found ourselves in this type of trouble, and she lives...in Conlin." Morgan thought for a moment. "I think."

"You think?" she exclaimed.

"Yeah, I...think," he said, fairly sure.

"We're spending some of the only money we have left for a train ticket to somewhere we're not sure we're supposed to go and is our only hope of survival?" she asked.

"When you say it that way, it does sound pretty bad," Morgan agreed.

"Great, my brother finally agrees with me, and it's about how we're both doomed." Katherine huffed.

"Well, there's a first time for everything," said Morgan as he and Katherine boarded the train, preparing to depart for Conlin.

The Train Chase

On the children's way to the train station, around twenty men who called themselves proud Grisham family members, had attacked the two children. A mysterious sniper had taken them all out smoothly.

The children were thankful and prayed to God, thanking Him for His protection.

"Is it over?" Katherine asked Morgan. Katherine thought about the Grisham family, hoping they were running out of men to send after her and Morgan.

Soon, the Grishams would need to start sending all of the scary employees from Rek Inc. to come after the children and end them.

"Revenge is a great motivator to do awful things," Morgan remembered being told, but money, cold, hard cash, was a greater tool to get people to do what you wanted.

Revenge and money, the Grishams were running out of one of them. Morgan hoped they would run out of both soon.

There was a large goon after Morgan and his sister. He was eight feet tall and full of muscle. He was a monster and mammoth beast compared to the children of the White Rider himself. He was also a goon on the payroll of the company, Rek Inc., who was funneled money by the Grisham family, to keep those who knew the truth in line.

What was the truth? The truth was that Rek Inc. was a morally bankrupt company with its filthy hands in nearly everything dark, twisted, and sinister in these United States.

This monstrous henchman had just boarded the train the children were on, and Morgan absolutely did not have a good feeling about this.

The big goon may have been tall and built like a rock, but he lacked plenty of sense and brains. Morgan knew he could use this to his advantage.

The henchman was a disgraced, dimwitted deputy who liked to play football but wasn't very good at it. His face hung like a droopy, sad dog. His name was Boris L. Ton.
People called him "Big BL" for short.

"Here he comes!" yelled out Morgan.
Katherine and Morgan had boarded the train and were getting settled into their seats when they saw Boris L. Ton, dressed all in black, a ginormous monster of a manly goon, emerging from a private black horse carriage and then boarding the train. The color went out of Morgan's and Katherine's faces.

"Wow!" said Katherine.

The black horse cart had the emblem of Rek Inc. on it.

The goon had been called especially to track down the two children wanted for the murder of a tall, dark stranger who had tried to kill them at the beginning of the story.

This series of events was not heading in a good and positive direction, the children thought. *What are we going to do?* they wondered.

The train had already started moving, and the giant goon was getting closer to the children.

While on the train, Katherine said sternly, "We have to get off this train now, Morgan. They'll be waiting to get us at the next stop."

"Who?"

"Who do you think? The Grishams!"

"What?!"

"The Grishams are coming. It's over for you," said the big, burly, not too bright man.

"No! It's over for you," Katherine said as she slammed the pan that she had, thankfully, packed in her luggage over the big man's head.

The large man fell over, out cold.

“When did you become so violent?” asked a concerned Morgan.

“I did today, by watching you, big brother,” was her reply.

“Oh, boy,” said Morgan. “We have to jump!”

“It is too dangerous,” said Katherine. “We will have to wait until the train slows down.”

“But by then, it will be too late,” said Morgan. “You heard the big Grisham goon. They’re waiting for us at the next train stop. They know where we are going, and we know that they’re there waiting for us. We have to jump. Now!”

“Okay,” said Katherine. “But I think we should first put the big goon in the caboose cart of the train and detach it. That way when he wakes up, he won’t be able to help the rest of them come after us.”

"Sly thinking," said Morgan. "When did you start thinking this way?"

"Spending all this time with my big brother, all of your bad habits are starting to rub off on me," Katherine replied.

"They're not bad habits if they keep us alive and protect us from the bad guys," said Morgan to Katherine. "If I have to choose between alive and the alternative, I think alive would be the best choice."

Katherine nodded in agreement with Morgan.

The children took the unconscious goon, tied him up, put him on the bottom of a covered mail cart, and pushed him into the back of the caboose. Then they went to the connector by the caboose, waited until no one was watching, and disconnected the cart.

Then they stayed on the train for a few miles farther and then jumped off the train, landing in a large hay field.

Whew! thought Katherine. *Maybe our luck is about to change.*

Their luck, however, did not change for the better.

When the train the children had been on finally arrived at its next stop, the Grisham men were upset to say the least. Especially since their large, solo goon was nowhere to be seen.

"They got to him!" said one of the Grisham men.

"Do not be ridiculous," said another. "Our man was four times their size."

"It does not matter," said the other Grisham. "These are no regular children. We must not underestimate them. They both have the blood of the White Rider."

The goon woke up alone in an empty caboose car to find he was all tied up. He wasn't very bright, but he was sure strong. At that moment, though, he was too weak to break free from his ropes that the children had put him in.

There were some unfinished meals in the cart on some tables in the train cart. He was hungry and saw there was some fried chicken and stew nearby that he couldn't resist.

The goon was getting ready to eat with his mouth on the bowl when he heard a roar in the distance. He ignored it at first, then he heard it again, much closer. He looked out the window and saw a very, very large grizzly bear headed towards the caboose.

He still was not too worried, because he thought the bear probably wouldn't be able to open the door to the train car. That's when he saw the door handle shake, and then turn, as if someone was trying to get in.

He heard more roaring at the door, then the roaring stopped. He took a deep breath and relaxed only to be shaken when the door to the car flew open and a huge, nine-foot tall bear came climbing in.

The goon was now beginning to panic, since he was still tied up and literally had no way to defend himself. Was this the goon's end? Had he been destined to become a bear's dinner?

The bear, however, seemed to ignore the large goon and was instead sniffing the selection of delicious, gourmet meals that had been left unattended in the train caboose. The bear walked over to one of the tables with multiple plates of chicken stew and sniffed each dish. Then he sat down at one of the tables as if he were a person and began to devour the dishes of still-warm, delicious chicken stew.

Many miles away, the children hoped this scary chase was close to being over, though Morgan knew better. Katherine wanted this whole situation to be far behind them or a part of some bad dream.

"We still have a ways to go," said Morgan.

Something told Morgan the two were just over the midway point of their adventure. The sun was setting fast, and they had to keep going.

Back in the train caboose, the goon was sweating. He did not know if he should join the bear for dinner with the risk of becoming dinner or get up and make a run for it. When the bear was done, he made his way over to the large goon, who was sitting in a chair next to the window.

The goon thought, *This is it. It is over.* But instead of bringing the death that he surely expected, the bear gave him a lick on the cheek and what could only be described as a real bear hug. The bear then turned around and left the train car.

In the caboose, the goon fainted from the stress of the bear stew situation.

The children of the White Rider continued forward on their journey.

Morgan remembered he had heard rumors, whispers of larger-than-usual-sized birds and other creatures in certain unexplored areas right outside Conlin's surrounding and bordering provinces. Of birds and bears much larger than had been around here in recent times.

One passerby Morgan had encountered whispered a story of a huge bird with a twenty-foot wing span. What was the big bird that the traveler had mentioned? Was it a huge falcon? Morgan couldn't remember. He had heard such stories when he was only three or four. Many of those memories now had faded.

If those reports of humongous white birds, or even falcons, were true…

Surely they had become extinct by now, due to the ambush and wave of new settlers pushing westward through the country.

"It would be amazing if we saw some giant falcons before this adventure was over, right?" asked an excited Morgan to Katherine.

"Falcons. Giant birds. How can you think about the wonder and joy of giant birds at a time like this? We are running for our very lives and my brother's daydreaming. How could you?" Katherine asked.

"Mother always said to stay positive and give thanks to God no matter where you are and what you're going through," said Morgan, eager to remind his sister that he did pay attention from time to time growing up. Paid attention concerning things that didn't just include hunting, wildlife, and fishing.

"I see. It's going to take a miracle to save us," said Katherine.

"Well let's get to praying," said Morgan.

The children of the White Rider started praying.

THE CANYON

Dynamite had been set and triggered by Rek. There were explosions as Katherine and Morgan were in the wagon that was being pulled forward. The two horses had one mission and it was to keep moving forward, keep heading directly on the path in front of them, keep going.

More explosions. They were from mines that were being triggered. But who was behind this, well, that didn't take much thought before the children both came to the same conclusion.

They looked each other in the face, at the same time, and at the same time as they were looking each other in the face, they said, "Grishams!" And they were right.

The Grishams rigged dynamite throughout the canyon and were triggering and exploding the dynamite as the wagon of Katherine and Morgan plowed through, barely escaping the debris, destruction, and carnage.

Barely escaping the smoke, barely escaping the devastation. Old man Roanan was not too far behind.

They didn't know it was Roanan yet, but it was. The old friend, the old sidekick, the old trusted and wise partner of the White Rider. He was on a white horse of his own, a huge horse, and it was riding up above on the canyon wall, paralleled with the wagon of the children.

Roanan was taking his time, watching over Chapman's children, Morgan and Katherine. He was taking out the Grisham bad guys, the Grisham men, one by one as they began to move closer and closer to where Morgan and Katherine were.

It was a sight to behold as the wagon with the children of the White Rider continued to move forward, barely escaping the debris and devastation as the Rek Inc. explosives continued to destroy the canyon all around.

Roanan was right there, picking off the Grisham men as they were on horseback.

Slowly they were getting closer, about to make a connection with the wagon with the children, and then at the last second they were picked off by the loyal ally of the White Rider, Dugg Roanan.

He was back! He was back to help.

That's who had saved the children earlier at the cabin. Who had stopped the tall, dark figure in time. That's who had been following them this whole time. It was Dugg Roanan.

The children were relieved to know who it was, but the same time, scared to death of what was ahead of them and what was behind.

"Why are they trying to kill us, Uncle Roanan?" asked Morgan.

"I reckon the mere fact of your existence is a perceived great threat to the Grisham dynasty."

"What?!"

"The success of *their* children is not a foregone conclusion, um-mm, inevitable, as long as you both are alive," Roanan told them.

Both the children nodded and agreed.

Run Them Off The Cliff

The elder Grisham who ran most of Rek Inc. knew of a massive cliff near the central Rek Inc. mining operation. You could not tell from topside that it was a cliff. It blended in with the rest of the scenery and horizon. You had to know it was there before you ever made it anywhere close to keep yourself safe.

The cliff was marked by several wooden signs to keep the Rek Inc. employees clear from danger. *Stay Clear! Stay Back at least a hundred feet!* the sign said. It was dangerous to be anywhere in the vicinity of the steep cliff.

In preparation of running the children of the White Rider off the cliff, the elder Grisham ordered all signs warning of the danger to be removed.

The White Rider children would either plummet to their doom off the cliff or stop beforehand and be apprehended and dealt with.

The ravine at the bottom of the now-unlabeled cliff was littered with years of Rek Inc. company trash, a dangerous dumping ground for the family of the Grishams.

The elder Grisham knew this would make a fine finale for his family's pain felt by the legacy of the White Rider. Push them off over the cliff, say good-bye to any future opposition birthed from the descendants of the White Rider.

“Run them off the cliff!” shouted the elder Grisham and boss of Rek Inc.

“That was the order!” yelled the Grisham family member, repeating what the elder Grisham had just said moments earlier.

“But they’re just children. We can’t, it’s not right,” said one of the concerned Rek Inc. employees.

The Grisham authority shrugged at the rebuke. “A little late to be developing a conscience, isn’t it, Ned? The bottom line is, do you want to get paid or not?”

All at once the Grisham employees began to nod and raise their hands slowly in murmuring and agreement.

“The children of the White Rider must not be allowed to grow up and cause our family and our great company problems. Their very existence causes an unstable element, threatening all we are, all we have built.” And with that, the Grisham family sent two more caravans full of family soldiers and Rek Inc. company men to find and hunt down the children of the White Rider.

The two caravans of villainous players chased the wagon with Morgan and Katherine all over what you would call creation.

They chased them through the back roads; they chased them through the valleys and through low tide rivers. The Grishams would not and could not stop, due to their fear and insecurity of what the children of the White Rider could one day become.

It meant the doom of the Grisham family for all-time if the corrupt dynasty of the Grishams failed to stop this new seed of a threat these children presented. It was nearly all over the dark plans the Grisham family had continued to grow in the darkness. Deep, twisted family plans for the future of the country.

The dark eyes of the Grisham family had had their sights set on the White House for many years. Though they had planned and plotted, their original plans had been thwarted and stopped by the survival of President Abraham Lincoln and General William Maxwell, the first White Rider.

The Grisham family had been behind the original Lincoln assassination attempt.

Back on the chase, the Grisham and Rek Inc. caravans had succeeded at chasing and forcing the wagon of the children of the White Rider to the edge of the desert company cliff.

The wagon came to a stop with nowhere to go.

Then, it happened. A white ghost appeared on a large, white horse. No one could tell who it was exactly, but they could feel the pain that his arrows, daggers, and bullets caused them. Their plan backfired.

Roanan arrived, just in time to help this White Rider ghost turn the tide on the Grisham and company men and chase almost all of the Grisham men, who had pursued them, off the cliff.

“This was a really bad idea!” several of the men yelled as they fell to their doom. Several men just jumped because they would prefer death to confronting the White Rider and his allies face-to-face.

Cowardness and deceit went hand in hand in the Grisham bloodline. A few men who leapt were able to grab vines and other artifacts sticking out from the side of the cliff.

Many of them stayed hidden there on the side of the cliff, until they were certain the White Rider ghost, Roanan, and the children, had departed from above.

“What was that?” asked the confused Grisham men who had survived the encounter.

“Was that the second White Rider? Was it Chapman back from the dead?” asked a few of the men.

The Grisham company men had all heard that Chapman's final battle was with a group of Apache from many years earlier.

Had Chapman been risen like Lazarus from the Bible? How was this possible? What did it mean? What were they going to do if that were true?

More questions than answers, more setbacks than progress had been made during the failed execution of this Grisham plan that had seemed foolproof just hours earlier.

Running the children's wagon off the cliff was supposed to mean that the children of the White Rider, not the best of the worst Grisham villainous men, would meet their doom.

The Parting of White Elk River Miracle

Roanan and the children of the White Rider—Katherine and Morgan—were up against what looked to be their doom. They had been attacked, they had been chased, and run all over the territories by the dark, twisted descendants of the Grisham family.

The Grishams were hellbent on finding, capturing, torturing, and then using the children of the White Rider, for their own selfish, dark, twisted goals. Ransom, etc.

Fortunately, Old Dugg Roanan, the family friend, was ready to step up, stop and prevent these descendants of the Grishams from following through with their plan of destroying the children of the White Rider.

Roanan had years of experience as a Bounty Hunter before he had turned to the side of light to help the White Rider, Chapman. He was up for the challenge, but now, they found themselves with nowhere to go.

Roanan, Katherine, and Morgan were in a wagon. They had been chased, and now the river kept them from being able to escape.

The river was up, it was high, and hope was anywhere but there.

Roanan made his way to the middle of the White Elk River, leaving the horses and wagon unattended with Morgan and Katherine inside. He told them to wait there; he was going to ask God for help.

Roanan made his way to the middle of the river and took his rod and slammed it into the middle of the water.

A miracle took place, much like one from the Old Testament in the Bible.

Morgan and Katherine looked at each other, startled and blown away by what was happening. Just as had happened to Moses in the story of Exodus, the faith of Roanan was honored by God, and the White Elk River parted.

It was a sight to behold.

Roanan immediately yelled out to Morgan, “It’s time. Come on, go! Go, get to the mountain peak!”

Morgan took the reins of one of the horses in front of the wagon and started off as fast as possible across the roaring river that had now parted. Morgan and Katherine were able to get across in time. Whenever they were across, they signaled for Roanan to come across.

Roanan shook his head. He knew he would not be following for much longer or helping to protect the children. At least not until the end of the story.

So he looked over and saw the sinister Grishams coming across. They'd already made it halfway across the parted river and were almost to Roanan.

Roanan knew they didn't expect him to do what he would do next. He nodded to Morgan and Katherine, and they knew what he was going to do. He removed the rod from the middle of the river, and, all at once, the river came down, splashing, consuming Roanan and the Grishams. All of their men—thirty Rek Inc. men—were washed away down the river, and the children of the White Rider had been saved once again. This time by the faith of Roanan.

THE MOUNTAIN RESCUE

The water dam had exploded making it unstable and the mountain was beginning to be wash away.

The children thought they had seen a white air balloon on the horizon, but weren't for sure.

There were larger falcons coming, ones not seen for perhaps many years, falcons so large they could grab a man and rip him from the ground, rip him from his horse, and take him. Well, at this time, there were two large falcons coming straight in and were attacking the sinister employees of Rek Inc.

Ka-kaaaaa! they called out.

The Grisham men went running. There was nowhere to hide, because if they went one direction, falcons would pick them off. If they went another direction, they feared bullets from somewhere else would cut them down.

If they went off the mountain, off the edge, then the water rushing under their feet would wash them away. Where were they to go? It looked hopeless.

Two large falcons were coming in and a large white air balloon arrived! They were going to give Morgan and Katherine a ride off the mountain peak that was now clearly doomed.

Right as Morgan and Katherine began to climb into the air balloon, here to rescue them, one of Grisham's men grabbed ahold of Morgan's leg. This sinister henchman wouldn't let go.

"Let go, let go!" yelled Morgan.

"No, never. You're ours! The legacy of the White Rider dies here! His children are doomed!"

Katherine saw this and thinking quickly remembered that she had a small assemblage of small stones and she began to throw them at the Grisham man holding onto Morgan.

The Grisham man who was holding onto Morgan's leg wasn't budging.

"You're mine! Give it up!" The Grisham man would not let go of Morgan's leg. Morgan began to kick him—but still, he wouldn't let go.

Finally, the Grisham man looked around to see all his other companions washed away by the flood. The dam had broken, the mountain was crumbling and washing away, even the children's wagon that had carried the children to this point, too, had completely submerged.

It was only the falcons and the large white air balloon bringing Katherine and Morgan to safety, along with this lone Grisham man that had survived and could not get the picture – only these remained.

Just then the Grisham man still holding onto Morgan pulled a small, miniature pistol from his boot and was going to point and shoot, killing Morgan and maybe even ending a few falcons, too.

Katherine continued to pelt the Grisham man with her small stones.

Finally, the man let go as Morgan kicked him in the face and as the Grisham man began to fall Morgan yelled out “I hope you don’t know how to swim!”

The Grisham man hollered “Owww!” There was nothing to grab onto as he fell in slow motion, the last of the scum of the Grisham family falling to their doom, to his death.

They hoped the body would not be found, but you never knew—the Grishams always found a way of resurfacing like plaque, scum, or floating debris that wouldn’t disappear.

At this time, the children were thankful. They were thankful God had provided and taken care of them. He'd used one of His most noble creatures, the white falcon.

They were celebrating—Katherine, Morgan, and Roanan—whooping and hollering as the balloon rescue attempt was successful and two large white falcons began to lead them to safety.

Praise God! they thought.

All at once, things took a turn for the worst. There had been one Grisham who had survived. This one Grisham had made it to the bank, whereas all the other henchmen sent from Rek Inc. had drowned.

The surviving Grisham was standing by himself on a large rock face that had not been submerged. He had a bow and arrow in his hand, but it was no regular arrow—it was a sharpened, sizable, steel metal arrow.

The man shot the giant, metallic arrow into the sky and struck one of the large white falcons near the passenger-filled balloon.

Then he shot another huge, sharp, silver arrow that collided with one of the enormous white falcons attempting to protect the escaping heroes in the balloon. Suddenly, the balloon dropped.

Morgan and Katherine fell into the new river recently formed, while Roanan tried to salvage his custom hot air balloon. Neither Morgan nor Katherine knew how to swim.

A feminine, white-robed figure reached down her hand into the water and grabbed ahold of Katherine. The same white-robed hand reached down and lifted Morgan up, bringing him to the surface. Both children, unconscious, were placed on the back of a white horse and carried on horseback out of the water.

There were two white horses.

One was the elder Gracie Gail Emerson's horse and the other belonged to the now newly resurrected White Dugg Roanan in his long white trench coat.

It was a good way to end the adventure of the children of the White Rider.

The children rested and recovered that day at Gracie Gail Emerson's house. They'd finally made it to their elder sister's house, peacefully surrounded by the serene ocean and horizon on the beach.

The children's mother met them at their elder sister Gracie Gail's home, returning safely from her urgent journey that had kept her away from them during this time. The children of the White Rider were excited to be reunited with their mother, Mary.

Once the children arrived at Gracie Gail's home, they had many questions for their elder sister.

Gracie was at first reluctant to answer, but soon the children's patience paid off and she was ready to tell them the story of how Gracie made it to where they found her to be, far from Conlin where she used to be a school teacher.

After giving the children some supper to help them recover from their very long, tiring adventures, their elder sister Gracie Gail settled in to tell Morgan and Katherine the tales of her adventures she'd had the past many years.

They were excited to hear new tales of the White Rider.

The above picture is artwork drawn by Morgan and Katherine summing up their adventure in *Children of the White Rider*.

AFTERWARD

These are the tales told to Morgan and Katherine by their elder sister Gracie Gail. The events took place several years after the story of THE WHITE RIDER NOVELLA, *Gracie Gail's Adventure*.

GRACIE GAIL'S PAST TRAGEDY

Michael Emerson, the husband of Gracie Emerson, had died. Michael passed away when the wagon he was riding in had an accident. The wagon wheel came off, and the wagon went careening into the river.

While attempting to get the horses free from the bridle and yoke, he was struck on the head and began to bleed out profusely. Then one of the horses took him down into the water, where Michael was unable to get to the surface for air. It was tragic.

Michael and Gracie had been married for several years, but had had no children from their union.

Several months after the funeral, many potential new suitors came from miles around to seek the hand of newly single Gracie Gail, the newest widow of Conlin.

Gracie wasn't having it. Gracie poured herself into her work at the schoolhouse with the children. She would not leave her house except for work and church. That was all.

Many suitors gave valiant efforts to win her hand, but those closest to her knew that that time in her life was over.

Gracie had lived her season of married life and knew in her heart that God was directing her to something new. What was that?

Answers would be revealed at a later time.

The New Courtship of Gracie Gail

A banker named Tobey Smutherland arrived in Conlin with the intent of wooing the widow, Gracie Gail. Everyone thought that since Gracie had legally changed her name back to her maiden name of Gail that she was returning to the life of a bachelorette, but when asked, she simply said it was in memory of her adopted father who had raised her in Conlin for most all of her life.

It was Gracie's dedication, and in remembrance of her father's faithful service to the people of Conlin as their only Reverend, that drove her to return to her unmarried name.

Tobey was a tad clueless when it came to most everything except for money.

Tobey was a financial genius, with weight issues, but with a woman, there was no end to the amount of misunderstandings that could or would be achieved with him attempting to court or date anyone or anything.

One day, Tobey Smutherland arrived at the school house where Gracie was teaching and began throwing rocks at the schoolhouse windows to get Gracie Gail's attention.

Smutherland threw seven rocks at the schoolhouse.

Gracie Gail was instructing her students in reading poetry that day. "Class, what are some of your favorite famous poems from history?"

Suddenly, the windows began to shatter. One by one, the windows in the classroom collapsed as the stones Smutherland was throwing struck their target.

"Sorry, I am very sorry, Miss Gracie Gail." Tobey tried to show some humility, but fell short repeatedly. "I suppose I did not know my own Goliath strength. My apologies, Miss Beautiful Gail."

The children, hearing this, began to giggle.

Hearing this, Gracie rolled her eyes and then went to one of the windows at the front of the schoolhouse near her desk. The children went to the other windows and began to watch the drama play out.

"I do believe I will be the one to successfully woo you and wed," Tobey declared. "Your heart shall beat by a rose-covered drum for the one and only Smutherland. In all the lands of this great country, there exists no other beauty and great flower as you! Allow me to pick you, my Buttercup Filled Flower."

Gracie Gail returned his words with deadly stares. Her face expressed that she was not impressed.

The school children, watching and listening, couldn’t help but laugh. The children thought it was hilarious. They made sure to go home and tell their parents.

You could say it was a dark time for the life of Gracie Gail, formerly known as Gracie Gail Emerson or Gracie Emerson, with this new era of romantic pursuit. She’d always had interest from one or two male suitors, including Michael, the sheriff, but never this many.

It seemed as though there were men coming from near and far, all over the territory, all over the region, all over the state, and several states away, attempting to be the next Mr. Gracie Gail. It was startling and a little disturbing, she thought.

Most disturbing of all was the leader of the pack. He was a very large, overweight gentleman, who loved chicken and eating it so much that he owned his own chicken company.

He was a little too proud of it, if you asked anyone who ever talked to him.

He loved his chicken, and he was coming to get a “Chicken Queen,” so to speak, to help rule his chicken empire.

It was disturbing, but the kids thought it was funny when this supposed “Chicken King,” larger than most, round “Chicken King,” who looked like a chicken himself, pelted rocks into the schoolhouse to get Gracie Gail’s attention. The children laughed. Gracie Gail told them to be quiet.

This King of Chicken followed Gracie home one day. Gracie found out that he knew where she lived, so she would stop at every single store and town business establishment, even stopping by the store and the bank, everywhere she could think to go so that her Chicken Pursuer would get tired, be hungry, and decide to go home and eat some chicken himself.

There were so many pursuers and potential suitors after the hand of the newly single Gracie Gail that, altogether, there were close to thirty that the children counted. Gracie decided, not really taking this seriously, to make a game of it. So she would invite them one at a time into the schoolhouse to have the children interview the suitors. The questions that they came up with were quite hilarious, and she could not help but laugh.

The children took very seriously the mission of finding a qualified suitor for her. They asked the most important questions.

"If you were a rock, what type of rock would you be? If you were a tree, how tall would you be, and would you be a good tree or a bad tree? Would you shelter the birds and the wildlife or would you fall over in a lightning storm and burn every one of your tree friends down?"

You know, really hard questions that need to be answered for marriage. Especially a successful marriage.

What in the world is the point of all of this? Gracie Gail thought to herself. She was trying to be nice, but it was getting out of control as the overweight "King of the Chicken" continued to pursue and bother her more and more.

Why would anyone love chicken that much? And she thought that even if she did give him a try, she'd always be second place to the chicken in his life. This continued for several more days.

Then one day, without warning, Gracie Gail left Conlin. Gracie had not told anyone where she was going. Gracie simply vanished.

The school children that Gracie had taught knew she had taken a white robe that she had been knitting since Michael, her husband, had died.

Gracie had worked on knitting this robe every day before and after school. The children thought she might be planning to go on a new adventure, like the one where she went to find the White Rider years earlier. Gracie had discouraged such talk.

When Gracie disappeared, many said that the courtship attempts that followed Michael's, her former husband's, death took a toll on her in many ways she would not speak about.

Being one of a handful of school teachers in Conlin, Gracie knew that if she were to leave town, the school house would be in good hands.

The madness brought on by this love and courtship hysteria business was too much for her. There was nothing wrong with being alone.

If that was what God was calling you to, then that was the path you were to walk.

It was as simple as that.

Those were the thoughts of Gracie Gail as she packed her clothes for the last time in the cabin she had grown up in. She packed the white robe, took one more look around as if to say goodbye with no idea when she might return.

Then Gracie closed the door to the cabin behind her, closing that part of her life. Michael and Gracie had lived in that cabin while they were married. The memories and time spent were at times overwhelming to the widow.

“Goodbye,” said Gracie to herself and to the cabin and then as she rounded the last building in the town of Conlin. “Til we meet again.”

Gracie had not only found her faith and courage and her real father in the wilderness, but she had found hope there as well.

Reminding herself of that brought a smile to her face for the first time since Michael had passed. What new adventure awaited Gracie Gail, only the Lord and fate knew for sure.

AVENGING GRACIE GAIL

There was a witness to the death of Michael Emerson. They saw the entire ordeal and they knew exactly what happened. Michael's wagon was sabotaged. Someone set out to murder Gracie Gail's husband...and they almost succeeded. Michael had survived.

Michael was washed down the river after the horse and wagon accident. Michael was found by a group of townsfolk and did not remember who he was or where he came from.

Michael did not remember Gracie Gail. Gracie was devastated, but when she thought it through, she realized that it was best to let Michael go. He had found a new life and a new wife.

But Gracie set out with the White Rider to find the man who tried to kill Michael.

It was Lucious Griswald who had attempted murder. Lucious had always had it out for Michael, thinking he deserved to marry Gracie instead.

Lucious was the son of a wealthy business man. Lucious loosened the seat of Michael's wagon and fed the horses spicy grain.

It was only a matter of time until a reaping arrived.

A CON-MAN IN CONLIN

"You know, you strike me as a man who is absurdly insecure about all things,"
said Reggie Clemons. The prideful and overbearing Reggie was projecting and asserting this onto Dugg Roanan, who he'd only just met a few moments earlier.

"I am a man of great talent, great wisdom, and I have great confidence in almost all things. My mother, she always told me so," Reggie continued.

Roanan wasn't buying what Reggie Clemons was selling, but he listened anyways to be polite.

"I graduated from the second school of Yale business."

Many who heard Reggie ramble on for hours weren't sure if he meant the school of business or the school of deception.

Reggie opened up a small store in the town of Conlin and leased for one month.

Reggie hired Roanan to help him move in.

"What's this?" asked a curious Roanan.

"What's what?" answered Reggie.

Roanan read the letter's return address was from a Mrs. Reggie Clemons. "I thought you said you were divorced from your wife."

"Which one?" asked Reggie. "I've been married many times. There are several Mrs. Reggie Clemons in the territories.
Enough about me, Mister Roanan. Tell me a little about yourself."

"Okay, I'm on a mission."

"A mission. Do you get paid?"

"Paid?"

"Serving the Lord is my payment."

"Ridiculous. Even working for the Lord, you must get paid."

"But my salvation..."

"The good book is very profitable."

"But in the Bible, Judas of Iscariot..."

"Was a very misunderstood and emotional man. So go on, what else does this mission entail?"

"I didn't get a chance to say, I'm going around and making things right for all who I did wrong when I did not know the Lord. Making amends for my sins?"

"And uh…how's that working out for you?"

"Actually, pretty well."

"You don't have to answer that, I'm sure it's awful."

"Well, no."

"Listen, I can help you make a tidy profit off this and advise you to never admit when you're wrong."

"I don't think that will be necessary, Mr. Reggie. I'm sure you have plenty to do here and besides, the township agreed to send Miss Evans to come help you once I moved you in. She has a knack for dealing with folks like you."

"Folks like me?" asked Reggie, offended.

"Folks that do a lotta talking, but there's not much coming out worth listening to, no common sense, just stupidity. Not much going on between the ears." Roanan pointed to his head.

"Well, how absurdly rude."

"No," said Roanan. "It's just…the truth."

Reggie scoffed.

"Oh, whatever you say, Mr. Reggie Clemons. Whatever you say."

Roanan left the business man alone. Reggie was appalled and upset, but it didn't take much to send him into a rage.

Reggie was more emotional than most church ladies in the territories, and one time it was reported that he stormed out of church when the preacher insinuated that God Almighty might be smarter than him.

Reggie couldn't believe such hearsay.

The nerve and gall of that absurd preacher.

The nerve.

A few days later, Miss Walker arrived at Reggie Clemons' Financial Office and Yo-Yo store.

Miss Walker was a short, headstrong twelve-year-old girl who had the spirit of a bull. More than a match for a big talker like Reggie Clemons. Miss Walker was also the daughter of Conlin's Mayor.

If you weren't on Mayor Walker and Miss Walker's good side, well, let's just say you'd better get there…quick.

Miss Walker was very upset when she stormed in Clemon's store one day, demanding a refund for eleven yo-yos that her and her friends had purchased. The yo-yos, as she declared, were faulty—defective.

Reggie Clemons was upset. "What did you do to my yo-yos, Miss Walker. I sold you perfectly good yo-yos."

"Your yo-yos, Mister Clemons, are faulty and I will soon be speaking with my father about your false advertising."

"What did you do to them, Miss Walker?"

"Myself and a dozen of my friends were practicing when we tried to walk the dog."

"What happened?"

"We tried to walk the dog and the dog walked off."

"What?!"

“The dogs walked off, Mr. Reggie Clemons and I have a mind to report you to the fair trade commission and local law enforcement.”

“Let’s just wait a minute here, Miss Walker.”

“No, you wait just a minute, Mr. Reggie Clemons. I’ve just about had it up to here with your false promises. Big empty promises.”

“How old are you? A young lady like you ought to be prepping for marriage so you can learn your place and stop your mouth from running from here to ten buck two.”

“And my father says a man like you should be prepping for the unemployment line, or more likely prison, yesterday and be on the first train out of Conlin tonight.”

“Miss Walker, now you listen to me...”

"No, Mr. Reggie Clemons, you'd better listen to me. The folks around here have been used, abused, stolen from, terrorized, conned, and been made to pay for other people's mistakes and you are dead wrong if you think we're going to be put through the ringer again by some absurd big and empty headed little hairless business con-man know-it-all from the coast who thinks they can come here and play us like a fiddle for an afternoon tea party. Have I made myself clear, Mr. Reggie Clemons?"

"Yes," Reggie quietly answered.

"I can't hear you, Mister Clemons?"

"Yeess," said Reggie louder.

"Good," Miss Walker said as she marched out of the shop and slammed the door.

THE LAST RIDER

On a beach in the east, a lone white-robed figure riding a white horse walked the shore line and approached a young girl, who sat crying.

"Why are you crying?" asked the white-robed figure on the white horse.

"It's over," she cried. "Haven't you heard?"

The white-robed figure shook their head. They did not know of what the girl spoke.

"The White Rider. He's gone," cried the girl once more.

The white-robed figure stepped down off their white horse and made their way to the girl. The white-robed figure pulled their hood back to reveal the face of a young woman with long, dark black hair.

"It's not over, it's only just beginning." The woman smiled.

The woman's name was Gracie Emerson Gail. The Reverend's only daughter, the daughter of Chapman the warrior White Rider, and the granddaughter of the first White Rider, General William Maxwell.

"It's you. You're..." the girl said, stumbling. Stuttering. She was beyond startled and excited.

The young woman in white nodded, smiled, and said, "The White Rider."

CHILDREN OF THE WHITE RIDER

EPILOGUE

Rek Inc. went bankrupt, for there was only one Grisham now left. Surely he would not carry his hatred and vengeance towards the White Rider's family on with him.

Surely his hate would not go on to carry forth the Grisham wrath against the Legacy of the White Rider…or would it?

Find out all this and more in the upcoming book, *The White Rider Legacy*, set in Alternate History World War II 1940s.

"And I saw heaven opened
and behold a white horse;
and he who sat upon was called
faithful and true, and in righteousness
He judges and makes war."

-Revelation 19:11 (NKJV)

The Holy Bible

If you enjoyed the world of
Children of the White Rider,
join the characters in the
exciting first Gracie Gail Adventure,
The White Rider Novella.

If you enjoyed the world of
Children of the White Rider,
join the characters on a
Christmas Adventure in
The White Rider: Christmas Rescue.

Fear. Hope. Faith.

Sean Hunt's The White Rider Storybook based on the award-winning *White Rider* film series is available now.

If you enjoyed reading the world of
Children of the White Rider,
join Chapman and Roanan on an adventure in
The Award-Winning Film:
The White Rider: Chains & Revenge

DEDICATED TO:

Jehovah God

Mom & Dad & Grandma

and

the next generation

to boldly

seek God's will

for their lives!

THE AUTHOR

Sean Hunt

A faith-based author and award-winning filmmaker, Sean Hunt wants to encourage young people to be passionate about their Christian faith and being creative in the arts.

Hunt's work maintains a clean entertainment policy on paper and on the screen.

Hunt wants to inspire everyone who reads or watches his works to dream big for the kingdom of Jesus Christ.

Hunt resides in the Midwestern Region of the United States with his wife, Kylie Hunt.

www.ingramcontent.com/pod-product-compliance
Lightning Source LLC
LaVergne TN
LVHW090530110826
845146LV00003B/1051